CONTENTS

Chapter 1
Egg or Eyeball?

3

I *am* a chicken. A baby chicken.

Like the baby chicken inside this book.

See?

egg   baby

Chapter 2
Spot

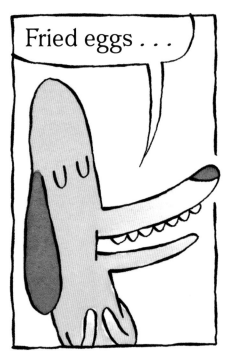

28

Chapter 3
Puff

35

37

Well, *hello,* Puff Huffman!

You smell good!

You smell great!

Oh, Spot. Puff Huffman said *no* because *you* did not say *please*.

Say *please*, and maybe Puff Huffman will come to your house for lunch.

Like this: *Puff Huffman, please come to my house for lunch.*

Chapter 4
Something Else

YOU TOO LOUD!
I WAKE UP!
WAKE UP BAD!

Chick! Spot! Puff Huffman!
Did you see that very big
thing *move*?

GO MY HOUSE! LUNCH! NOW!

Oh, Something Else. You did not say *please*. Like this: *Please go my house* —

Oh, brother.

But that egg could be my brother! That egg could be my sister!

We have to sit on it! We have to keep it warm!

No, Chick, *no*! That is not an egg! It is an *eyeball*!

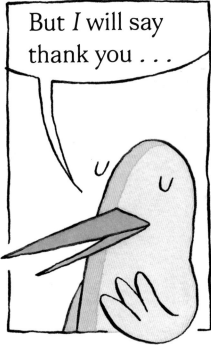

Oh, Kelli Huffman!
Oh, Frank Huffman!
Oh, oh, oh!
This book is for you.

First published in Great Britain 2020 by Walker Books Ltd
87 Vauxhall Walk, London SE11 5HJ

2 4 6 8 10 9 7 5 3 1

© 2020 Cece Bell

The right of Cece Bell to be identified as author and illustrator of this work has been
asserted by her in accordance with the Copyright, Designs and Patents Act 1988

This book was typeset in JHA My Happy 70s

Printed and bound in China

British Library Cataloguing in Publication Data: a catalogue
record for this book is available from the British Library

ISBN 978-1-4063-9247-0

www.walker.co.uk